Love notes for my inmate Merry Christmas in White

December /
Romantic Ramen
Noodles

Take that bowl of Ramen and imagine draping those noodles over my breasts and between my legs. They are warm and wet, now nibble and suck them off of my body.

December 2
Morning sex

Imagine me walking the dog first thing in the morning wearing nothing but a sundress and sandals, as the breeze makes my nipples hard. Back at home I pull off my clothes and lay on the bed with my cell phone waiting for you to call and talk me to orgasm.

December 3
Commissary Treats

Pick up that pack of lollipops. Go back to your area. Unwrap it slowly. Suck on it & lick it imagining you are between my legs.
Call me.

December 4
"You have 1
minute
remaining."

Before we are disconnected, tell me all the ways we are going to have sex the day of your release.

December 5
Sex in a Tent

Don't just describe what you do in the tent you make for privacy, describe your tent. ~~Imagine~~ being inside of me and doing push-ups using only your inner pelvic muscles.

December 6
Escape

Picture us in a missionary position. Start rolling and sliding like we are going under a fence.

December 7
Love Notes

All the things I would whisper in a hug. All the things I would scream in bed.

December 8
Visitation

What are visitations
for if not for making
me ready for you? I
am tempted to
crawl over the table
and sit in your lap.

December 9
No 3rd Party
Calls Allowed

The phone lady leaves me wanting to bounce up and down, sitting on the side of the bed with you inside of me. She can listen.

December 10
1, 2, 3.....

1 2 3 I want you

inside of me.

4 5 6 let me suck

your 6

7 8 9 it will be more

than fine.

December 11
Chow

Ever heard of the Upside-Down Cake position? Picture the kitchen table, me with the upper part of my body on it with you supporting my lower back and bum while you stroke inside of me.

December 12
Shakedown

While you are getting shook down, I'll be shaking myself up thinking of you. In the shower with the shower head between my legs.

December 13
Contraband Love

On the bed on my knees, one hand gripping onto the headboard. Spreading my knees further apart with my other hand I'll start with my nipples, moving down until I find myself all wet and wishing you were here.

December 14
Lock Down

Lock me down with your body on top of mine. I'll lock you up with my legs wrapped around your back and arms around your neck.

December 15
Bag Meals

If I were making
these, there would
be love notes stuck
in with the sandwich.
(With graphics of
our favorite
positions)

December 16
Photoshoot

Lingerie, bikini or leather. Your choice. Outside, in the car....tell me what you want.

December 17
The Wheels on
the Bus

I hate when you go on the bus. Waiting for your call with my phone balanced on my breasts and only a pair of sexy panties on I'll rub myself through the lace or satin making the panties wet and me writhing on the bed.

December 18
What's causing this moan?

Can you tell what I am doing or with what toy to cause a moan? Let's see!

December 19
Strip Tease

Tell me the music to put on. Listen while I describe my "routine."

December 20
Phone Sex Bingo

Phone Sex Bingo

Scream	Standing	Touch	Rub	Lingerie
Champagne	Spank	Massage	Beg	Silk Sheets
Missionary	Moan	Ties	Toys	Scream
Wine	Panties	Sex	Oil	On Balcony
Crotchless	Suck	Slower	Candles	Scratch

See Bingo Cards at the end of the book. Can we have phone sex and track the words on our cards? Prizes for the winner!

December 21
Role Play

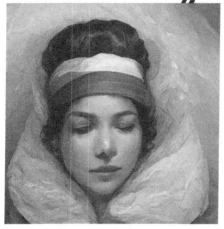

I feel hot. Tell me how you are going to check my temperature.

December 22
Co-Author

Let's write our own hot and steamy romance. One page at a time. The mail room ladies will enjoy it!

December 23
Strip Poker

I'll shuffle the cards, deal 2 hands. Piece by piece I will describe my losing hands. You tell me what to take off.

December 24
Recreating
Titanic Scene

Walking out of visitation, a quick glance up to the guard tower. Images of you and I leaning against the railing making love. The wind in our hair, cheers from below.

Phone Sex Bingo

On Balcony	Bubble Bath	Slower	Chocolate	Lingerie
Thong	Moan	Spank	Kiss	Panties
Suck	Missionary	Nipples	Champagne	Rub
Crotchless	Scream	Standing	Beg	Scream
Handcuffs	Ties	Toys	69	Wine

Phone Sex Bingo

Panties	Massage	Silk Sheets	Nipples	Ties
On Balcony	Handcuffs	Kiss	Wine	Spank
Crotchless	Toys	Rub	Oil	Chocolate
Scream	Touch	Slower	Suck	In Front of Window
Standing	Candles	Beg	Lick	Bubble Bath

Phone Sex Bingo

Oil	Panties	Missionary	Standing	Suck
Thong	Spank	In Front of Window	Lick	Slower
Toys	Silk Sheets	Chocolate	Scratch	Crotchless
Sex	Massage	Bubble Bath	Scream	Beg
On Balcony	Doggie	Nipples	69	Rub

Phone Sex Bingo

Scream	Standing	Touch	Rub	Lingerie
Champagne	Spank	Massage	Beg	Silk Sheets
Missionary	Moan	Ties	Toys	Scream
Wine	Panties	Sex	Oil	On Balcony
Crotchless	Suck	Slower	Candles	Scratch

Phone Sex Bingo

Lingerie	Scream	Champagne	69	Spank
Wine	Crotchless	Suck	Handcuffs	Panties
Nipples	Scratch	Beg	Bubble Bath	Sex
Touch	Lick	Kiss	Scream	Chocolate
Candles	Missionary	In Front of Window	On Balcony	Slower

Phone Sex Bingo

Lingerie	Bubble Bath	Standing	Ties	On Balcony
Candles	Chocolate	Thong	Sex	Suck
Nipples	Crotchless	Panties	Massage	Missionary
69	Toys	Spank	Oil	Lick
Moan	Silk Sheets	Handcuffs	Touch	Rub

Phone Sex Bingo

Scream	Candles	Rub	Moan	Sex
Standing	Suck	Touch	Nipples	Toys
Doggie	Panties	Thong	Slower	Chocolate
Lick	Oil	Beg	Missionary	Silk Sheets
Kiss	Crotchless	Lingerie	Massage	In Front of Window

Phone Sex Bingo

On Balcony	Scream	Thong	Kiss	Handcuffs
Toys	Candles	69	Beg	Scream
Ties	Spank	Silk Sheets	Lingerie	Champagne
Standing	Panties	Oil	Missionary	Slower
Bubble Bath	Scratch	Sex	Chocolate	Crotchless

Made in the USA
Las Vegas, NV
25 November 2022